THE FADED
EMOTIONS

Published By

The Faded Emotions

Written by Multiple Authors

Copyright ©

MULTIPLE AUTHORS - POETRY WORLD ORG 2020

ISBN (Paperback) - 9789389959475

First Edition : 2020

Book Design by POETRY WORLD

THE FADED EMOTIONS

Compilers

Aman Prasad Shaw

Surya Chakraborty

CONTENT

Desiderium 10

Edge of Winters 13

Be the change 15

Long Distance Love 17

The Pitch Sound Of Silence 20

Soft wings 22

Love : nectar or poison 25

Scars and voices 27

No Matter the Roses You Bring Me Now 29

Life with facts and figures 31

The dark creation of god 33

Peace 35

An encounter with my soul 37

One Summer Night! 40

I wish I would have captured! 42

A time in past, love shimmered in my heart 44

In the memory of beloved 46

Colours 48

Angel Eyes 50

The untouched touch 52

Your love fades away 54

Me and Moonlight 56

Twin Flame 58

Embarking on Solace 61

Castle of Dreams 63

The holocaust 65

While I witness my own funeral pyre 68

Walk with Me! 70

Beautiful Thing 72

Hooked Up With Fantasizing Love 75

The Faded Emotions 78

That Very Love 80

वो खुले बालों वाली लड़की 84

हर हर्फ़ शिकायत लिख दी थी 86

सच्चा प्यार 89

हुआ होगा...92

दिल का दर्द 94

प्यार मोहब्बत 97

खूबसूरत इत्तेफाक..99

दोबारा ये मोहब्बत बेइंतेहाँ कहाँ होगी... 101

शाम तुम फिर आना… 104

बिछड़ना 106

AARTI SRIVASTAVA

A 20-year-old geek, describes herself as a 'fangirl', 'avid reader', 'a proud hufflepuff', and 'someone who is forever in search of new keys to the multitude of worlds existing inside the written word'. You will usually find her hidden in the corner of her room, or under a tree, somewhere no one else can see, her head miles away on a magical journey that she desperately seeks.

DESIDERIUM

A goodbye said forever ago
Haunts my nights still.
Something left unsaid,
Someone still holding hostage,
My soul.

I cannot escape it,
Nor hide,
From the voice,
Whispering,
Even beyond dawn.

We all have regret,
Some big, some small,
And letting go I feel,
Is neither right nor wrong,

But I refuse to forget.
Even though
I live with this ache
In my heart,
I know,
That if I choose
To forget and move on,

I may again fall prey
To the despair
Of the love long gone.

So I choose,
To remember, always.
So that if I come upon
A love that is even
A tenth of yours,
I cherish it,
And hold on,
Till my final fall.

AKANKSHA SINGH

Akanksha Singh, a graduate and resident of Lucknow has indulged herself into reading and writing since a very young age. Writing things down is her heart time job. She also works as a content writer for an NGO and co-author of 4 anthologies. As an artist her works have been published on various platforms.

EDGE OF WINTERS

On the edge of winters,

The Sun is in the blanket of fog,

The little drew drops on tree's top,

Sitting by window feeling the chill,

With a hot coffee mug on the sill,

The scene so dramatic,

Like a fairy tale franatic.

But down the valley in the darkest street,

Lies a boy without any treat,

With matted hairs and shaggy pants on,

He lies on knees moaning for warmth.

But just as the warmth wrapped him around,

Pats him on the back with sympathy dumbfound.

Holding the hands of happiness risen,

He walked to the new world crossing the horizon.

On the edge of winters laid the leaf fallen from trees.

ALISHA KHWAJA

Heya! My name is Alisha and I'm in 11th standard now.
Writing has been my first love, always and forever. I even
love to interact with people. I started my writing profile this
year and earned quite a few accolades. Also, Paulo coelho
fan fiction were always my niche.

BE THE CHANGE

I sat by the shore in murky night full of stars sprayed,

Mesmerised by the ripples on the moonglade.

Then I heard a discordant melody in the sky,

The sussuration of constellation from so high.

As the stars spoke to me,

About the bitter truths and melochonies

Of women painted roughed red,

Or stabbing to reach the one's end

Hatred so profound in blood and bone,

Or desire unleashing the madness in return.

My soul, like porcelian is so contrite

Shameful of burgeoned sinful sights

Probing for the lost humanity

Or maybe a dash of sanity.

But the stars catch my thickening fear

And fills my vacant eyes for me to reach conclusion

That I'm not such a human

For the intiquities to cage

And to stay strong to be the change.

ANCITA OSHIN D'SOUZA

Hailing from Udupi of Karnataka, AncitaOshin Dsouza is 23 and currently pursuing Chartered Accountancy in Mangalore. She had conceded her B.com and B.A in Konkani literature. She writes for local magazines and bulletins. She is interested in poetry writing, music and public speaking. She is the co-author of the anthology 'The Penned Emotions'

LONG DISTANCE LOVE

A ray of light on the beautiful flower,
Made it bright in the morning hour;
Resembling you its bloomy look,
At your memories I then got stuck.
And when in the evening it faded,
You from my sight got vanished;
Making me realize you're not here,
And I again started missing you, my dear.

Cool breeze when I sensed,
By its coolness I got wrapped;
Your embrace then I felt,
There and then I did hault.
And when the sun changed its form,
To make the environment warm;
You released me from your hug,
And I again started missing you, my drug.

Clouds were all set to shower,
To give life to the dried well and river;
Just as you bring life in me when I'm down,
To make me smile when I frown.
And abruptly when the lightning struck,
Giving me an unexpected shock;

To the reality it brought me back,
And I again started missing you, my hunk.

How many days, months or years,
Will my eyes produce tears?
In your thoughts, your memories,
To burden me with worries.
No matter how hard, how long,
Your love will always keep me strong;
Though away you are, very far,
To my heart you're always closer.

ANKITA BRAHMA

Ankita Brahma is an evolving amateur poet with commerce as her background. She aims to inspire masses through her poetic skill on life. She seeks nature to base her poetries. Her thoughts clubbed with her imagining skill helps her to derive the real essence of emotions and life to the readers. She believes that words are magical for it impacts life of both the writer and the reader in real time. Her motto for life is "Connect through words for it's a wand to manifestation."

THE PITCH SOUND OF SILENCE

Only hearing will put you to failure,
For feelings is its nature.
Only one who felt it could interpret its forms,
Of highs and lows on its onset reforms.

Sound of internal fight, hides.
Veil of laughter resides outside.
Sound to make peace within form clusters,
Of subtle smiles that screams inside.

Arms of isolation traps,
With echos clenching in surrounding depth.
Feeding slowly of illusions into mind,
Of never ending trails still undefined.
The crowd calls for escape,
Giving short liveliness instate.
Still lasting longer than ever,
For disguised in solace for them instead.
An hour, a day, a month, a year which passes...
The silence of unfelt emotions,
Transforms the one who holds them.
For it steals the old one for new changes.

ARSHIYA MITTAL

I am a coder and writer currently pursuing CSE in Big Data.
I have achieved success in many field such as poetry,
coding and others such as MUN, academic achievments. I
have good leadership qualities and good communication
skills. I have my own book published named "The passages
of life" available on amazon and flipkart.

I always need to explore more and untill the work is not
done, I don't get satisfied that makes me good at my work.

SOFT WINGS

The eyes full of drops,
In hands holding the props.

Her body badly scratched and cracked,
Her soul was in someone else sac.

She was in dark, no one to give her feather,
Scared of the barks, that made all around terror.

In vaccumed room she was there,
All in smoky, dark there was only fear.

Losing hope for everything,
She was wounded for doing nothing.

Finally, she got out of smokes but did't get the wings,
No one listened to her sayings.

She is also the citizen of the golden world,
Asking from all 'where are the wings have you heard?'

Searching for her wings, the needle moved further,
After a long time she got some hope rather.

Her search was now over,
She got the wings with soft feathers.

Thinking about her dreams so far,
Thought of that she have to travel above the stars.

No one was there to wipe her tears,
But she stood and overcame her fears.

Saying to everyone, don't you dare
to get puzzled and afraid,
This world is a big bad market trade.
Make the monsters ignited by your power,
Make them all feel a loser and
then take a peaceful shower.

Now she has soft wings to fly,
To inspire everyone not to cry.

Much to tell and write in her diary,
Because she has to fly like a fairy.
She wants to be up above in the sky,
And shine like a diamond up so high.

ARYAN MISHRA

My name is Aryan Mishra. Currently fighting with corona and online class, I'm in absolute love with poems. From Lucknow, I'm usually busy finding words for my vocabulary in my books. I would search for ideas around me when people are busy facing screens.

LOVE : NECTAR OR POISON

Love is a metaphor,
Praises my day,
Love is an irony,
My nights say,
War waged in wordings way,
Reality met and told that gay.

If love is a kite,
Honesty is the wind that makes it sway,
Love is a tryst,
That's what makes it weigh,
Love is to worship,
Depends on your reason to pray,
If you're searching for body,
It's a filthy chase,
But if you demand for soul,
That's what makes you an ace.

Not everyone who says,
Does stay,
Not everyone is blasé,
About hearty plays,
Few hands will yet hold you in haze,
Few eyes still have blaze.
And if it's still confusing,
Love is about finding the one,
Who'll get you out of this maze!

All I heard was an echo
An echo of a bewildered voice
Seeping into my mind
As I've heard it before

As I reached closer,
It reminded me of someone
Someone who is bold and brittle
Someone who is pretty and pretentious
Someone who has the most awful scars

I saw her,
Right in front of me
While I was looking into the mirror
Flabbergasted she whimpered
Looking at her distraught self

A splendid imagery of how beautifully
She could've lived
Pricked her into reality where she was
Wilted and withered like a dead rose
With no thorns dangling onto a tattered cadaver

All she pleaded for was to be thrown out of the darkness
Engulfing her body
And her soul that's stained in blood of misery!

- JOSHI RAMYA

BATTULA JOSHI RAMYA TEJA

Hello I'm Joshi Ramya, an amateur poetess. I love writing poetry especially in dark genre and also about love. I'm astonished by the profound caricature of words forming into a beautiful poem.

SCARS AND VOICES

All I heard was an echo
An echo of a bewildered voice
Seeping into my mind
as I've heard it before

As I reached closer,
It reminded me of someone
Someone who is bold and brittle
Someone who is pretty and pretentious
Someone who has the most awful scars

I saw her,
right in front of me
while I was looking into the mirror
Flabbergasted she whimpered
Looking at her distraught self

A splendid imagery of how beautifully
she could've lived
Pricked her into reality where she was
Wilted and withered like a dead rose
with no thorns dangling onto a tattered cadaver

All she pleaded for was to be thrown out of the darkness
engulfing her body
And her soul that's stained in blood of misery!

FATIMA RIAZ

Fatima, is a young artist with a passion to write and a power of winning hearts with her inked sheets.

Fatima (2004) belongs from a very civilised family based in Lahore, Pakistan. She is pursuing her FSc in Pre Medical and aims at becoming a successful doctor in the future, whom her parents could be proud of. At such a ripe age, she has got her work published in "World on Trial: The Earth's Grand Vengeance" , where she expresses her poetic sentiments about poverty. Later, she got featured by the same publisher; @witchesnpink in "Flash!", where she presents a trifling and nail biting short story. Then in "In Which Poetry Breathes Life". She is also a writer in 3+ anthologies under Poetry World Org. We must say, Fatima has come a long way!

NO MATTER THE ROSES YOU BRING ME NOW

If the sky calls upon me
And pulls my breath away;
And I, by your side,
No longer stay
But the love for thee,
Will forever be.

If tomorrow's Sun didn't open my eyes,
May you lead a thousand cries
And regret for weaving the truth,
A little less.
I would not return.
Though to caress your tears.

If tomorrow's breeze touch'd my face,
A cold blow.
The spring unfold'd but the gardens,
Refus'd to bestow!
No matter, the roses you bring me now;
I wiltered long ago.

If tomorrow starts without me,
And yet I keep turning my head
In search of you, calling my name.
Atleast come,
Come! One last time
See me turning into dust!

GRACY ANGEL N MARAK

Hails from the Scotland of east,

Student of literature.

LIFE WITH FACTS AND FIGURES

Walking through fire,
With weary heart;
Will it melt the core?
None know what the branches of life hold.
Ev'ry Soul doesn't walk on one track;
For the roots of life,
Holds Summer And Winter.

"Seek the eternity"
Set the wings free,
And' let the instinct fly.

Cross the desert of pain,
Swim through the ocean of Love;
Walk hand on hand with patience,
'Let the journey of Life '
Set the quest for Rainbow.

Like the portrait of Truth,
Coming out of the well;
Life sets the tone of voice
With naked Wisdom,
To flaunt the fact,
Not the Sugar coated Illusion.

Erase the wicked desire
Unchain those Melody,
Dance to the Beat
And sing to the rhythm of Life.

GURLEEN KAUR

My Name is Gurleen kaur. I am 20 years old. I was born and brought up in Delhi. My Hobbies are writing, painting and dancing. I am pursuing my graduation in tourism studies and french language. I aspire to become a famous writer.

THE DARK CREATION OF GOD

Can stab her in a womb
If born, will lock her in the coop
To fulfill their lust, they can tear her rags
O God! Help me!
Humans are evil.

Make an elderly women vagrant for her generosity
Where a son brutally kills his father for his currency
They are the darkness in the bloom
Where everything is now dim

To chase one's dream, they can witch others spirit
To gain happiness, they can give others darkness
The garden of God now became the graveyard for all
Will the race ever change?

In this cruel world where blood is hungry for blood
Now god even don't want to own this earth
What happened to humans?
Do they have a heart?
Or have they became the demon?

IRTISHA DEY

Cheesy, Round.

Rambles, mostly.

Loves F.R.I.E.N.D.S, pockets, hills, rains, letters, poetry, bookmarks, balconies, carnations and starry nights.

Started writing since she was 8 and aspires to write a full novel someday.

Likely to be found laughing with strangers and writing stories on them.

PEACE

Holding onto every amorous thought

Feeling his heated skin against mine

Having the impassioned rawness I sought

So carnal yet so divine.

The lingering warm breath on my skin

The raw passion in his gaze

As he enters me, our souls unite

Two bodies with passion ablaze.

Our desires fed; we lie exhausted

Healing each other's broken piece

The bond we share is reincarnated

This is how we make peace.

JYOTI GOGIA

I am an educator by profession and scribbler by passion.
Capricorn by luck and writer by chance. I have been
scribbling since my school days. Whatever I write, is
something that my heart pours out. Words line-up
themselves and I don't need to put any effort from outside.

Her passion towards pen scribbling induced her to write
sincerely and now she is trying that her write-ups should
reach everyone.

AN ENCOUNTER WITH MY SOUL

On that cozy evening, I was lying inert

When that sweet voice distracted my ponder.

I was astonished and took a quick spurt

To find the clue of that voice yonder.

A girl I found standing on the window

She turned and I saw a replica of mine.

"Who are you?", I asked and scared though

"I am your soul", she replied with a smile.

You have stopped listening to my cries,

Neither you listen to my words instead

So I come here to make with you allies,

The kin you have thought to be dead.

You are an exuberant valorous woman

With a mellow heart full of emotions,

To define yourself you don't need a man

Who fills your heart with grief and commotion.

Benovelence is an act of generosity,

You showed up many a times although

Yet letting some people allow to be witty

And spearing your soul with sharp arrows.

You've become so busy finding love

You've lost all connections with your soul.

You kept yourself that piece apart shove

The only one that completes you whole.

O! My dear mistress, I know you are hurt

Your heart is broken and back is stabbed.

Still you're worthy of cleaning this dirt

Wiping your tears, healing scars that jabbed.

I am here to let you reminisce your worth

You are a woman, one in million

All you forgot is to love yourself first,

While seeking goodness in a filthy spun.

KAJAL MITTAL

Kajal Mittal. A CS aspirant. Born & brought up in Maharastra, India. Following her heart by penning down emotions Instagram handle : @prettylittlesayings99

ONE SUMMER NIGHT!

One Summer Night,

Surrounded with the fireflies,

Having you by my side,

There we both decide,

Together let's fight,

For all the love we sacrificed,

Looking at each others eyes,

Falling for every moment we had it right,

A feeling of paradise,

Holding hands together we recite,

Our love is eternal bliss and to be precise,

You're the one for ever in my life!

MAHIRA KHAN

I am Mahira Khan a fisheries science student from Madhya Pradesh. Writing is equivalent to breathing for me. I love penning down whatever I feel and wanna express in the form of poems, short write-ups, stories and articles. I am a budding instagram writer who is looking forward to explore more in writing. Have a happy reading.

I WISH I COULD HAVE CAPTURED

I wish I could have captured
When last my grandpa held my hand
The last time he hugged me
Or the last I saw him smiling with his fam.

I wish I could have captured
The time I played in his lap
The time we laughed together
And the time he scolded me and I ran.

I wish I could have captured
When he taught me to read
To add and subtract
Or to stand and speak

I wish I could have captured
You in every moment.
As who knows
You will leave silently, leaving me broken

I wish I could capture you now
When I think about you
I just can't accept
I won't be able to see you anyhow.

I had captured you in my heart.
Your words, your lessons and your dreams.
that I'll surely try to conque till last.
I know God took us apart.
But you are forever in my heart.

MELODY PHIJAM

I'm a Science student from Manipur who finds solace In
poetries and trying to ink my own.

A TIME IN PAST, LOVE SHIMMERED IN MY HEART

Like the sea shimmered in the sunlight,

Inompleteness abandoned me in delight

When you hugged my tearful soul tight

And kissed my wounds under the starlight

Healing them with your douceur so bright

I waited for you everyday under the mistletoe at twilight

For nothing tasted more pacifying than your presence

I loved you like the ocean loves the sky.

A time in past, love shimmered in my heart.

Now that you've faded away from my life,

I wreath myself in smiles

Inhaling the fragrance of bygones.

MOHSIN ALI

I'm Mohsinali, a student of First year from Budgam, Jammu and Kashmir. Since the days of childhood, writing has been my passion, which brought me up in the survey of life. Writing to me is a nourishment, which energizes my soul with immensity of passion. It's all about transformation of heartbeats into poetic verses along the scent of breath. I'm inspired by nature, beguiled by life and embossed by the colors of voyage.

IN THE MEMORY OF BELOVED

In the memory of beloved,

I drank the intoxicated wine,

Under the dark cloud

When sun didn't shine.

The moon was near,

And cup in hands tight,

The soul was exalted to bear,

The sip at night.

His fragrance went around,

Which attracted me towards the tavern,

It wouldn't have found,

If his scent didn't fall in.

I couldn't see his face,

If that sparkle of grace

Wouldn't have fallen on,

In my void lawn.

NABANITA SARKAR

I am Nabanita Sarkar and I am a great enthusiast for novels and poetry. The beautiful and heart touching words are enough to melt my soul. And slowly and slowly I also found my way into this world of poetry.

COLOURS

The empty sky of mine so dull and grey,

A hollow world of despise, hate and fray.

So you came into my life,

Painted the empty sky blue,

And trust me all these feelings are so new.

Melted this forbidden heart,

And kept it nice and safe.

You came into my life,

Painted this icy blue heart,

To the deepest shade of red.

When the tears of my eyes started to rain,

You danced under the storm to know my pain.

So you came into my life,

Gave my sunset a touch of violet,

A perfect harmony of blue, red and dark scarlet.

NEHA PRASHAR VERMA

I am a Business Development professional, an ardent traveller, a military wife, a mother to a naughty princess and above all a budding writer who loves to tickle the brain and churn out new ideas.

ANGEL EYES

Deep as the sea, clear as the skies,

Dark as the night, are those Angel eyes.

The eyes so innocent, and the eyes so wise,

Still so determined, and yet so nice.

Oh! they are filled with such a charming force,

And yes, -with hope, -no need to tell, of course.

Always, they seem like a sweet surprise,

Really really strong, are those Angel eyes.

The eyes of mercy, the eyes of love,

And finally the eyes of honor all above.

Just a glance is enough, for them to cast the spell,

What magic do they have? God only can tell.

Watching them only, the sun sets and rises,

Such a thing of beauty, are those Angel eyes.

And when they join, the million dollar smile,

Bewitching, they became, unearthly for a while.

When I look at them, I could always see,

My world full of love and my world so free.

POOJA BADKUL DAS

I am Pooja Badkul Das, the author of this poem. I have a passion in writing and I'm a youTuber too. Being a teacher my youTube videos consist mainly of educational and motivational webinars. I find pleasure in writing poems and sharing them. I would be pleased if in future I get this chance to share my work/content again.

THE UNTOUCHED TOUCH

I sense the grace of his untouched touch,

His gestures kind and caring much,

It made me get his feelings through,

So gentle that I never knew

I trust these vibes because energy doesn't lie,

The soulful impact will never die,

Wanna stay close to his heart forever,

Parting cannot be an option ever

He keeps his words like brave and bold,

His faith in me has the power to hold,

He stood with me from the very first day,

But a recent art of him took me away

He says me we will together fly high,

No words are enough to praise this guy,

I peeped into his eyes and you know what I found,

No lust but love all around.

PRIYANKA VEGDA

I am a freelance model in Film industry as a junior artist since more than 5 years. I am an passionate creative freelance writer, blogger, storyteller, influencer and a spiritual soul.

YOUR LOVE FADES AWAY

Broken heart to trust again,

Not an easy task, so think again.

Words just keep on flying,

Action creates more impact on trying.

Yes, I'm alive in the chaos,

You don't bother anymore,

But yeah I still exist.

Wait, wait and wait,

Oh god! It feels like a cage,

Yes, I do exist.

You came up like a hope,

I accepted you like a dream

and a scope.

Your words flew away,

Your promises faded away.

But you don't care anymore,

Even if I exist or die.

SAADIYA AFZAL

SA (@herunspokensoul_sa_) is an amateur writer trying to turn her dreams and thoughts into words. She is currently pursuing her doctorate of pharmacy. She is an ambivert with lots of enthusiasm and wishes to spread her beautiful awestrucking magical aura everywhere as much as possible.

ME AND MOONLIGHT

She stood alone amidst her chaos,

With no sight of any better tomorrow ...

She cried her pain away all night,

With the bluest of blue type of sorrow..

In the darkness of this world ..

She found her best friend..

The one that stayed with no "THE END"

Soothing her heart..

Making her feel the world can also be full of art

Giving her peace without any fight..

Staying with her until she was alright

Making her life a little more bright

It was none other than the mightiest moonlight..

That saved her every other night..

SAMRUDDHI SHARMA

Hey there! I am epigrammatist and a writer. Published in many anthologies. Who loves to express her ideas in the form of writing.

TWIN FLAME

Somewhere, somehow

In another dimension.

Where time and energy

is a reality Or still an illusion.

Where the two flames are said to be twin

And two souls as the part of one.

I and you is just a part of one soul.

The bond between us will never break

No matter, whatever happens.

even if we are existing in different

Physical form, space and time.

We surely meet, as we are

inherently same being.

I am you, you are me

altogether we are one

we are us. The two pieces of one .

No matter if we exist

in other dimension or same.

The frequencies, time and energy of two universe synchronized.

Our paths may cross and we will meet again in afterlife.

The flames of soul

Illuminate that bright

That we the twin discover

Ourselves even in the dark.

Through the path of universe, through the speed of light we found

ourselves and meet again. Distance and time doesn't seperate us

our souls are eternally connected and influence each other.

We are the twin flame in quantum entanglement. We were always

meant to be. Even in DARK or in LIGHT.

The love, Adoration and bond

Isn't complicated it is just as simple as

Quantum physics.

SATAVISHA MISHRA

My name is Satavisha Mishra and I am from Bhubaneswar, Odisha. I am a management graduate and currently pursuing MBA in HR domain. Being born and brought up in New Delhi, I had keen interest in reading and writing. Hence in Bhubaneswar I started to work as a freelance content writer for city based media organizations. This pandemic came as an opportunity for me to function as an editor for a pan India famous publication company. Other than writing, dance, cooking and painting keep me engaged in leisure time. I aspire to release my own book of poetries in near future.

EMBARKING ON SOLACE

Sagged with heap of questions
That were numerous,
To be answered
Even in a state of consciousness.

My heart endeavors
To stow away those questions
However, they seem to slip from my grip;
Just as sea shore's sand.

Swimming, in the passage of time
Answers which were most sought,
Reached me draped in translucent robes,
Robes of unheard echoes.

Yes, the echoes happen to be mine
Emergent of all anguish
Later locked inside
The chambers of my heart.

Fathomable,
As answers disrobe gradually
Guiding me on the path,
Where I meet my new self.

It's an amalgamation
Of me and my soul,
Ready to walk
Thresholds of solace.

SHEETAL

Writing is my passion.. creativity is my soul food...I'm not perfect but my creations are always better with a touch of imperfection....

CASTLE OF DREAMS

Get along with the lines of life
Shout out loud to be acknowledged
Gasping for air and breath away
Searching in the middle of nowhere

Steps taken to get along soon
Was that a good path waiting?
Beloved you wanted me to be myself
But something drifted apart from the core

Running on a journey of life together
Never would have been the same
Turning up to the mark of the day
Castle of dreams brought smile on my way

Myth of the soul are unheard waves
Floating around in the middle of the night
Holding knots of emotions inside-out
Sudden change of heart beats for the same...

SHRAMANA GANGULY

Shramana Ganguly is an aspiring author, also as a student of English literature she strives to dig deep into the history of literature and composes poems and writes short stories. She leaves sparkles mixed with ambiguous endings and lures bookworms into an amazing charm which is felt throughout her works.

THE HOLOCAUST

The holocaust

The dead soldiers dressed in wounds

Panting as hiccups bled blood

They told their stories of war

That died with them in the altar

Of despair.

The boy who soiled his pants, while

Playing over the strip of land

Has now gunned down the opponents

For reasons he never found.

The baggy uniform smelling like roasted meat,

Was giving away burnt hopes to live.

So was his hair that his mum washed with tender care

Now filled with dirt, the dirt of the holocaust

That soiled million hearts

He stooped down to find

His hat, his recognition mingled with dried blood

Of where he stood with bleeding ears

That pained with the exploded sound

His hands wet with sweat and dirt, lined with blood

Whose was it? He will never know.

He killed lumpsome and left none

The treachery, for discrimination, for power

That will now not palliate the wounds of these soldiers

All gone!! All gone!!

From arms and legs torn to pieces

From gas leaks that paled the young man

They died, collapsed in whose fight?

The duplicitous ones who gained fame

The autocracy that trembled history

The wars revived, the heroes spoken of

The politicians fowl ignorant piece of dirt

They just shouted war cries, inspired soft bosoms

Who never knew war was the cry of the pessimism

Until they climbed over hills

To find death drooling as it fed on human corpses.

SOUMILI BISWAS

Name- Soumili Biswas

State- West Bengal, India

Currently pursuing 12th standard

Stream- Humanities

Hobby- Writing and Reading

WHILE I WITNESS MY OWN FUNERAL PYRE

Ashes, smoke, woods piled up in a row
Oh! What's that stinking smell?
Blazing rays shooting up into the sky
Orange, yellow, red
It's a mess
I go ahead and ahead
To find what's that...
My eyes sticking out,
I see 'Me' wrapped in the blazes
What's that?
A corpse...
No,
One being burnt alive
And that's me..
I witness that girl shrieking
Oh my dreams in flames!
Oh my aspirations!
Oh my happiness!
Oh my freedom!
Oh my desires!
Thousands of hands strangulating the poor Dalit girl
And I stand there,
Witnessing my own funeral pyre
'My Own' funeral pyre..

SRUTHI KALIYAPERUMAL

A writer and a youTuber, who loves to see world in a new dimension. A girl next door who appreciates the dawn as well as the dusk of life. Literature, History and Mathematics have always had my heart. A happy go lucky girl.

WALK WITH ME

When the shimmering wave shares,

The unusually coarse shores,

When the luscious green leaf seeks,

A kiss from the sun on its cheeks.

When clouds strike a conversation,

On the basis of mountain's narration,

When my footprints stand alone,

In the wait of a pair of its own,

All I want my vision to see,

Is You Walking right beside Me.

You promised that we would never separate,

Unfortunately, time refused to co-operate.

There you fly with the rhythm of the wind,

Along the path which doesn't seem to end.

But when my footprints stand alone,

In the wait of a pair of its own,

All I want my vision to see,

Is you walking right beside me.

SRUSHTI DANGUR

Srushti Dangur is a Physical Therapy student by profession. She likes to pen down her feelings and flames of life. She has also been a co-author for many anthologies. Apart from her medical interests she likes to read novels and watch movies. What lifts her up in any situation is good food. She dreams of touring the world and inspiring minds through her writings. She is also a nature and animal lover who aims to make this world a better place. You can find her writer's page on Instagram @thesharedpen318

BEAUTIFUL THING

You tried your best
To define my boundaries
But I dwell in the skies
A wide blue yonder
Limitless, intangible.

Just by the twilight
I blow a gust of wind
Yet so gentle, humble
The leaves embrace
Some fall, rustling
I engulf the fallen
In my seamed brown lands.

Sometimes I ravage
Whatever tries to stop me
Yes, I am a cyclone too
Rebelling amidst
The colors of a rainbow.

Even as an island
I'm all surrounded
With gallons of salt chucks

And waves crashing upon rocks
Rocks as massive as mountains
Gorgeous waterfalls
This is my climb.

I render you
With warm morning kisses
A beam of bright yellow
Myriad of emotions
Intense, tempestous feelings.

Your wanderlust mind
Swinging, unstoppable mind
Meanders sublimed
Oh! The lush green beauty!

My divergent boundaries
You've confined in a map
But the blue yonder defies
All limits, gravity
I am divine.

O mortal! Let me live too
Let there be serenity, unpolluted
For we are a beautiful thing
Together, always.

SUCHISMITA GHOSHAL

Suchismita Ghoshal from Malda, West Bengal is an internationally acclaimed poet, professional writer, scribbler, published author, professional book critic, storyteller, columnist, former copy-editor at NotionPress Publishing, content writer, creative writing professional, nature lover and a change agent & former Worldwide Ambassadors' Coordinator for Global Youth Leaders Network. She is now a registered member of Global Youth Network. She cherishes her partnership with various publication houses of India & abroad. Suchismita also aims to heal people with the majesty of her words. She is an environmental activist too who brought reality to her dream as her debut book named "Fields of Sonnet". Her recent releases are "Poetries in Quarantine" and "Emotions & Tantrums"

HOOKED UP WITH FANTASIZING LOVE

Turbulences in my mind,

Tossing you up and never been so kind.

Louder my soul speaks whereas your lips

Dripping juice of seductive lime.

An impulsive urge to make you mine

Your muscular body reflects the perfect shine

And I gift you the best kisses like wine.

Anguishes made me stronger than ever

Each touch of mine makes you shiver.

You linger to my ears slightly touching my belly,

My unadorned desires invoking the lines of Shelly.

Trying to decipher the mantras to make you wild,

Where electrifying gazes make you shield.

You crave for more and more, quite teasing my breasts

And I don't want to spoil the tiniest moment of love in haste.

Troubles come to my navel arousing

my lecherous wishes

As your tongue proving to be the God of sexual bliss.

The night paints a bluish canvas with the aroma of cozy love

And my mouth sips every drop of your manly pride.

Gluing your body with mine and pricking your fingers inside my

vagina,

You leave me to the extreme point of fantasy with the tender

dignity.

Love me baby, take me higher than the limits of this sky,

Paste your divine lust and make me sway.

Dismantling every layers of our shyness,

We devoted our entities with the gel of fineness.

Infatuation blending into the adorations

Plucking the sweetest nectar of our dedication.

We end up leaving no parts of our bodies untouched,

As our connections do not have any glitch.

Cleansing the ambiguous thoughts from our kind,

Our last drop of french kisses opened up the windows of fresh

wind.

SURYA CHAKRABORTY

Surya Chakraborty a boy from middle class family who was born on 20th August 2000 in West Bengal Kolkata, has completed his higher education from Kolkata and now is running behind the degree on computer based education and dreams to get a good job on computer sectors to fulfill all dreams of his parents, whichever they have sacrificed for him.

Other than these he also loves to express his feelings as well as experiences through his Quotes and Poems. He hopes that you all can relate his poems and quotes with your life and can understand its feelings. He believes that God gifted him such a precious capability which helps him to reach others through his writing. If you want more quotes and poems then follow him on his social media account:-

Instagram Account: - Chiefsurya007

Facebook Account: - Surya Chakraborty

THE FADED EMOTIONS

One fine day of a beautiful summer I lost everything except my sense of humour, and a painful smile still somehow hanging from my face, as I lost everything without having any tress.

Stress levels are gradually increased and I started to lose myself, all my craziness has faded away and all I have that nothing on my way. All my emotions are buried under my pains & my tears are hiding under the rains, finding the way where to go as my stations are also galop by trains.

Slowly slowly swallowed by the diseases, now life turned out to be a great sin for me where situation says me to quit it up and still I found myself fighting. Everyone has became my enemy where my own shadow used to be my best friend. This shows how the tears got dry and the emotions have faded away.

TABASSUM HASNAT

Tabassum Hasnat, a freelance writer of short form fictitious genres. She has her own personal blog on the global platform of Story mirror Pvt Ltd. She is aiming to seek a wonderful opportunity to enhance & apply her writing skills in a dynamic workplace.

THAT VERY LOVE

I have seen love idly loitering,
bare inches away from one's soul,
before seamlessly seeping at times -
bit by bit, and at times all at once -
into the pits of that very soul,
while caressing the core of it,
with one lovable ardency.

All I hadn't seen was that selfsame love,

shattering right into those pits,
leaving behind its once solacing shards,
to shred that very soul apart -
with no reach of one restful retrieval.

Until now, when I could see it -
That one fervidly yet foregone love,
Sickeningly stepping away in defeat,
While I strive hard to scavenge -
for the slain scrapes of my soul,
which remained disoriented in such dilapidation,
Devoid of any dreamlike redemption.

POETRY WORLD ORG.　　　　　　　　　　　FADED EMOTIONS

ABHIJEET KUMAR

Myself- Abhijeet kumar

I'm from darbhanga, Bihar.

I'm pursuing my graduation

Writing is my hobby and I write for my own pleasure

My favorite poet is daagdehlavi and john eliya.

वो खुले बालों वाली लड़की

वो खुले बालों वाली लड़की, जिसपे मै मरता था,

हाँ याद आया मै प्यार भी बेहद उससे करता था।

वो थी पूरी सफ़ेद और रंग मेरा साँवला था,

हाँ याद आया मै फिर भी बेहद उसके लिए बावला था।

नज़रे चुरा के वो देखती तो, मै भी उसमें डूबा गहरा था,

हाँ याद आया मेरे दिल में उसका ही पहरा था।

एक दिन चलते चलते उनसे मुलाकत हो गई,

हाँ याद आया ना होने वाली जो थी वो हमारी बात हो गई।

बात करते करते मै पूछ बैठा कुछ ऐसा था,

हाँ याद आया उसको पसंद कोई मेरे जैसा था।

वो खुले बालों वाली लड़की

AKSHAY AJAY BEHRA

Presenting Akshay Ajay Behra author of the book "एक प्याला इश्क़"and Co-author in 25 different anthologies with 10 world record holding anthologies, Herewith Akshay is a silver medalist national level hockey player and have participated in 26 different national championships in his entire sports life and Akshay is now pursuing Post Graduation Diploma in Journalism & Mass Communications.

हर हर्फ़ शिकायत लिख दी थी

हर ग़ज़ल अधूरी कर दी उसने, आज क़्यामत लिख दी थी,
एक ख़त था और कुछ पन्ने थे, हर हर्फ़ शिकायत लिख दी थी।

की उसने ज़ुल्फ़ें चोरी, मक्ता पायल लूट गया,
फिर ग़ज़लों को रही शिकायत, थोड़ा हिस्सा छूट गया।
गजरा बेबस रहा सेज पर, मुरझा सारे फूल गए,
तुम यूँ उलझे थे ज़ुल्फ़ों में, चूड़ी कंगन भूल गए।
अर्से बाद कहा भी कुछ तो, सारी आफ़त लिख दी थी।
एक ख़त था और कुछ पन्ने थे हर हर्फ़ शिकायत लिख दी थी। ।

थीं उम्मीदें तारीफ़ों की, बस आए शिकवे हिस्से में,
तुम काजल लिखना भूल गए, न पिछले वाले किस्से में।
दो मेहंदी वाले हाथ हमारे, ख़ुद के सीने पर लिखते,
जो बहा ले गया सागर अपना, मिट्टी वाला घर लिखते।
बेचैन अधूरे वादों की, लाचार सी हालत लिख दी थी,
एक ख़त था और कुछ पन्ने थे, हर हर्फ़ शिकायत लिख दी थी। ।

चमकीले कपड़ों में शायद, एक परी दिखाई देती थी,
और चश्मे में मेरी आँखें, कुछ बड़ी दिखाई देती थी।
मैं ताने सुनकर ग़ुस्से में, कहती थी क्यूँ तुम खम्भे हो,
मैं कद में छोटी नहीं हूँ शायद, तुम ही ज़्यादा लम्बे हो।
बहुत नमाज़ें अदा हुईं, रूह तक में इबादत लिख दी थी।

एक ख़त था और कुछ पन्ने थे. हर हर्फ़ शिकायत लिख दी थी। ।

मेरे हाथ का खाना खाकर, हुआ जो अपना हाल लिखो।

वो पहली रोटी जली हुई, और कंकड वाली दाल लिखो।

फिर से उँगली चखकर देखो.

बाक़ी मेरा स्वाद है क्या.

वो चावल की पहली सीटी. और तीखी पूरी याद है क्या।

कुछ कल के धुँधले ख़ाब हमारे. आज की आदत लिख दी थी.

एक ख़त था और कुछ पन्ने थे. हर हर्फ़ शिकायत लिख दी थी। ।

वो देर रात को छज्जे पर. चुपके से आना कौन लिखे.

उस झुकी नज़र का बाहों में. घुलकर शर्माना कौन लिखे।

जो की थीं चाँद की तारीफ़ें. तो दाग भी सारे लिख देते.

अच्छा लगता गर ग़ज़लों में. कुछ ऐब हमारे लिख देते।

फिर हक़ से कर लो बयाँ ख़्वाहिशें. और इजाज़त लिख दी थी.

एक ख़त था और कुछ पन्ने थे. हर हर्फ़ शिकायत लिख दी थी। ।

लिखो कहाँ बेबस थे हम. और कहाँ जुदाई मार गई,

कहाँ इबादत झूठी निकली. कहाँ ख़ुदाई हार गई।

मैं नहीं जानती हाल तुम्हारा. आख़िर मेरे बाद है क्या.

वो तुमसे मेरा लिपट के रोना. आज भी तुमको याद है क्या।

एक ओर ज़माना लिक्खा था. एक ओर मोहोब्बत लिख दी थी.

एक ख़त था और कुछ पन्ने थे. हर हर्फ़ शिकायत लिख दी थी। ।

AMAN PRASAD SHAW

Aman Prasad Shaw born in West Bengal, Kolkata in a middle class family on the 27th day of March, 2000. Whose father is a Business man and my mother, a housewife. The major part of his education was done in Kolkata. Currently he is working in an office and his future planning is to do something good for him and his parents to fulfill their dreams. That dreams which they have sacrificed to make his future.

Other than these he also love to express his behind the scenes look on his Love Life in the form of Quotes and Poems. It helps him to modifying him better than yesterday. The quotes and poems he is writing is specially for those who are in love with their partner or whose heart's are broken from inside. I hope that you all can relate his poems and quotes with your life and can understand its feelings. He believe that it is a god gift's with which he was born with. If you want more quotes and poems then follow him in his social media account:-

Instagram Account:- "poetamanprasadshaw",
"love_life_2718"

Facebook Account: - Aman Prasad Shaw (Mr Perfect)

सच्चा प्यार

उस एक दिन जब बातें शुरू हुई आपसे

लगा कुछ तो अलग सा है आप में

लगा कुछ तो नया सा है आप में

फिर रोज़ की बातें होती गईं

और यूं बिना सोचे पिघलता रहा मैं उनमें

यूं ही बिना समझे फिसलता रहा हूं रास्ते पे

हां पता था मुझको उसी रास्ते जा रहा हूं जहां गम बहुत है

पर गम की क्या बात यहां आपका साथ ही बहुत है,

उस दिन जब पहली मुलाकात हुई आपसे

लगा जैसे मैं खुद को मिल गया.

फिर आपका मुझको चुनना

चूमना मुझको गले लगा कर

कसम से मेरे अंदर कुछ तो कमाल कर गए

बहुत दिनों से शांत मेरे मन में सवाल कर गए

फिर मिलना हुआ और मिलते रहना हुआ

आपकी बातें आपकी आंखों से पढ़ना हुआ

आपको ढूंढ कर आप में ही खोना हुआ

सच सिर्फ यह है कि प्यार सिर्फ

आपसे कई हजार बार हुआ

फिर हुआ कुछ बुरा

शायद ऊपर वाले की मर्जी थी

आपका मुझसे काफी दूर चले जाना हुआ

मेरा आपको हर दफा याद करना हुआ

और हर आंसू के बाद भी दुआ में उठते हाथ

और झुकी नजरों में सिर्फ आपको और

आपकी खैरियत ही मांगना हुआ...

BHUMI VARMORA GOPANI

I am from Morbi, Gujarat, Bharat.

I am not a professional writer but I just like to pen down my feelings.

I am basically gujarati, so gujarati literature is in my blood as my father is also very interested in literature.

I am a house manager who just wants to connect with the world by my own words.

हुआ होगा..

पता नहीं कब, क्यूं, कैसे और कहाँ हुआ होगा!
ये इश्क जैसे बयां होता है क्या वैसे ही हुआ होगा?!!

आज बेपनाह सी यादों की सीलवटो में खड़ा मिलता है वो
कैसे मान ले ए इश्क कि टूटकर जब लौटा तु तो ना रोया होगा

आधे भरे हुए पैमाने की मदहोशी की कसम तुझे
बारिश में भीगा जब सारा शहर तब तु सूखा रहा होगा

ए इश्क हाथों में पकड़ा वो गुलाब भले ही सूख गया हो
इत्र से ज्यादा पसंद आज भी तुम्हें वो सनम का महकना होगा

बेखयाली नैनों की आंखमीचौली में रूमानी जो वादे किए थे
वो बिना अल्फाजो वाली अनकही बातें अकेले में तु भी याद करता होगा

मशहूर तो हम हुए ही ए इश्क तेरी मेहरबानी से महफ़िल-ए-महोब्बत में
सिसक सिसक के जब हम रोयें "जय" तब दर्द तुम्हें भी तो हुआ होगा...

MONIKA OBEROI

I am Emotional, Loving and Caring person.

I love cooking healthy food.

I love painting, drawing and doing art and craft.

I love to write poetry and short stories.

I am a good teacher.

I am a youtuber.

I am a blogger.

दिल का दर्द

दर्द को छुपाये रखा है,

टूटे दिल को बचाए रखा है।

लबों पे ताला लगाए रखा है।

बेवफाइयों को तेरी सीने में दबाए रखा है।

बड़े बे मुरब्बत हैं हाथ ये उठते हैं

केवल दुआ देने के लिए।

आबाद रहे वो जिसने

चिराग मेरी हस्ती का बुझाए रखा है।

बढ़ता हूँ आज भी इस उम्मीद से

शायद कोशिशे कामयाब हो मेरी

क्योंकि नाउम्मीद होने में क्या रखा है?

मालूम है खुशियां नहीं हैं मेरे दामन में

पर फिर भी किस्मत आजमाने में क्या रखा है?

मेरी तकदीर लिखकर भूल गया खुदा भी मुझको,

पलटकर देखता भी नहीं, किस हाल में मुझे रखा है।

पर फिर भी हँसते हैं हर जुल्म पर उसके

क्योंकि रोने में ऐ खुदाया क्या रखा है?

देखनी है मुझको हद उसकी सितम ढाने की

क्योंकि घुट-घुट के जीने में क्या रखा है ?

दिल में शोले भरे है लाख हमने,

उसने भी तपती रेत पर अंगारें बिछाए रखा है।

हार हम भी न मानेंगे, कर ले आजमाईश वो जितनी।

देखे हम भी जीत जाने में क्या रखा है ?

गिर-गिर कर भी फिर उठ जायेंगे हम

क्योंकि थक कर टूट जाने में क्या रखा है ?

तबीयत ही कुछ है ऐसी अपनी

मिल जाए जो यूँ ही,

मज़ा उसे पाने में क्या रखा है ?

NIDA BANGI

Myself Nida Bangi, I Love To Write & Love To Spread My Words.

प्यार मोहब्बत

एक सुकून कि राहत है,

तन्हाइयों में तेरी आहट है,

तेरे साथ से रोशन क्षमा है,

आसमान में बुलंदी लेता जैसे कोई परवाना है,

आंखों में कुछ सुनहरे सपने है,

तेरे साथ जो बुने है वह ख्वाब मेरे अपने है।

NITIKA SHARMA

I am Nitika Sharma. My Hometown is Heaven as I am a mountain girl. A coder in an IT firm with a poetic mind is something I do for living. Undying love for travelling, italian, acoustics, coffee and optimistic souls is something that defines me.

खूबसूरत इत्तेफाक

खूबसूरत इत्तेफाक ही है मोहब्बत

जो नाजाने कितनी मर्तबा टकराई है मुझसे

कभी आँखों से कुछ कह गयी

कभी बेबात बातों से दिल ले गयी

कभी तुम्हारा हर पल मे साथ होना भा गया

कभी लम्हों मे मुझमे तुम्हारा यूँ खोना

मुझे मुझसे ही चुरा गया

खूबसूरत इत्तेफाक ही है मोहब्बत

जो कहते कहते चुप करा जाये

खूबसूरत इत्तेफाक ही है मोहब्बत

जो नाजाने कितनी मर्तबा तुमसे टकरा जाये

OMISHA KUSHWAHA

I'm OmishaKushwaha from Prayagraj, Uttar Pradesh.
Basically, I'm a student, doing my graduation(1st year) in
journalism and mass communication from
BanasthaliVidyapith.

दोबारा ये मोहब्बत बेइंतेहाँ कहाँ होगी...

एक दूसरे को पहचानते, पर फिर भी नहीं जानते थे,

हम अंजान थे, नादान थे, अब वैसी दास्ताँ कहाँ होगी।

मुसाफ़िर थे, राह में मिल भी जाते थे अगर,

तो बिन बोले गुज़र जाते थे, अब ज़ुबाँ ये बेज़ुबाँ कहाँ होगी।

हम नदी के दो किनारे थे, सोचा न था मिलेंगे कभी,

हमें इस तरह मिलाने वाली वो नाँव, हमारे दरम्याँ कहाँ होगी।

बदलते मौसम में, कभी बरसात का आना तो कभी बादल छा जाना,

एक बार ये वक़्त ढल जायेगा, तो फिर से ये उम्र जवाँ कहाँ होगी।

तूफ़ान का क्या भरोसा करना, हवा चली अगर,

तो जगमग ये दीये बुझ जायेंगे, तब रौशन ये शमाँ कहाँ होगी।

घंटियाँ नहीं बजेंगी मंदिर में, पर शोर तो होगा ना दिल में.

कहीं नज़र लगी रिश्ते को, तो शांति आसमाँ में कहाँ होगी।

कुछ समय का खेल, तो कुछ ज़माने की साज़िश होगी.

मकाँ तो होगा रहने को, पर पहले जैसी वो खिड़कियाँ कहाँ होगी।

आँखों में अश्क लिये, दोनों की मजबूरी पत्थर सी होगी.

नर्म तो होंगे हम, पर हमारे बीच नज़दीकियाँ कहाँ होगी।

क्या चीज़ है तलवार, उससे कई गुना ज़्यादा धार होगी.

और लोग तो करेंगे ही वार, अब ये दुनिया इतनी मेहरबाँ कहाँ होगी।

फिर एक दिन शहनाई बजेगी, पर कोई और आपकी साहिबा होगी.

तक़दीर उसकी होगी, मेरी डोली आपके लिये रवाँ कहाँ होगी।

SRUJAN HIRAL GAURANG

Srujan is a student of humanities, having shy & introvert personality; but she loves to observe different types of people and to understand their behaviour. Reading, writing and dancing are her hobbies. Having a background of classical dance, she can get into different characters and feel various emotions which she tries to pen down. Also she is founder of writer's community @fiftyshadesofwriters on instagram. You can find her as @sruju_25 and @fiftyshadesofwriters.

शाम तुम फिर आना...

एक शाम तुम फिर आना, हर लम्हा हम जी जाएंगे।

बीतता वक्त, भले चलती घड़ी,

हाथों में हाथ थामे हम ठहर जाएंगे।

आज की तेज मचलती लहरों में,

हम कल की कश्ती चलाएंगे।

साथ बैठकर एक दूजे के,

हम वह पल फिरसे दोहराएंगे।

एक शाम तुम फिर आना, हम वो सारे वादे निभाएंगे।

शोर भरे इस शहर में हम,

खामोशी से तुम्हे पाएंगे।

जीया है जिसे ख्यालों में बार-बार,

वह पुरानी सफर पर जाएंगे।

प्यार हुआ था जिस पल हमें,

वह लम्हा महसूस कराएंगे।

एक शाम तुम फिर आना, हम नए डोर से बंध जाएंगे।

बात अधूरी ना रहे, हर पल को वक्त से चुराएंगे।

अल्फाजो से बयां करके नहीं,

हम आंखों से लब्ज सुनाएंगे।

छुटी थी कहानी जहा से अपनी,

फिर वहीं से आगे बढ़ाएंगे। एक शाम...

PRATIK SONAWANE

Pratik Sonawane, He is a merchant navy officer. He completed his nursing and Nautical science. His hobbies is reading, writing and playing cricket.

बिछड़ना

तुमसे बिछड़ने से पहले तेरे करीब आ जाना चाहता हूँ

तेरे साथ बीते हर पल को याद कर उनमें खो जाना चाहता हूँ

मोहम्मद अधूरी रह गई सोच कर कभी निराश मत होना.

तेरी मोहब्बत ही है इसलिए आज भी मैं तेरे नाम से जाना जाता हूँ...

हमारा मिलना मुक़द्दर में नहीं था

फिर भी तुमसे मुलाकात हो गया

ज़िन्दगी भर साथ नहीं तो क्या हुआ

कुछ पल है सही तुमसे मोहम्मद की बात हो गई

तुम्हारे एक बुलाने से फिर भाग चले आऊँगा मैं

तुम्हारे साथ बिताए हर पल को याद कर मुस्कुराऊँगा मैं.

और जब कभी किसी चीज़ को जरूरत है ना तो याद कर लेना.

तुम्हारी जरूरतों में तुम्हारी जरूरत बनकर आऊँगा मैं...

बिछड़ना

हम दूर है पर दिल के पास रहेंगे,

साथ बिताए हर पल हर लम्हें कुछ ख़ास रहेंगे,

दूरियों से फ़र्क नहीं पड़ता,

बात तो दिल की नजदीकीयों से होते है,

आपसे मिलना तो हमारी किस्मत थी,

वरना मुलाकात तो जाने कितनो से होते है...

मेरी ज़िन्दगी में कुछ ख़ास है वो,

मेरी तन्हाई में मेरे साथ है वो,

फ़ासला कुछ दूर है उसके मेरे बीच,

पर ख्यालों में ही सही मगर दिल के पास है वो...

POETRY WORLD ORG.   FADED EMOTIONS